Thomas Comes to Breakfast

The Rev. W. Awdry
Illustrated by Robin Davies

Dedicated to the memory of
Stuart James Eggenton (1992-96),
a little boy who loved to have his breakfast with Thomas.

Thomas the tank engine has worked his branch line for many years. "You know just when to stop," laughed his Driver one day. "You could almost manage without me."

**Thomas didn't understand that his Driver was only joking.
"Driver says that I don't need him anymore," he told the others.**

"Don't be so silly," said Percy.
"I'd never go without my Driver,"
said Toby earnestly. "I'd be frightened."

"Pooh!" boasted Thomas. "I'm not scared. Just you wait and see."

It was dark in the morning when the Firelighter came to light the engines. Thomas drowsed comfortably as the warmth spread through his boiler.

He woke again in daylight. Percy and
Toby were still asleep.
"I'll give those silly stick-in-the-muds
a surprise," he chuckled.

He felt steam going into one piston, and then to the other.
"I'm moving! I'm moving!" he whispered. "I'll creep outside
and stop. Then I'll wheesh loudly to make them jump."

Thomas thought he was clever, but really he was only moving because a careless cleaner had meddled with his controls. He tried to wheesh, but he couldn't. He tried to stop, but he couldn't. He just kept rolling along.

"Never mind, the buffers will stop me," he thought hopefully.

But that siding had no buffers. The rails ended at the road.
Thomas' wheels left the rails and crunched the tarmac.
Ahead of him was a hedge, a garden gate and the
Stationmaster's house.

The Stationmaster and his family were having breakfast. It was their favourite one of bacon and eggs.

"Oh horrors!" exclaimed Thomas as he shut his eyes and plunged through the hedge.

There was a crash, the house rocked, plaster peppered the plates. Thomas peered through the broken window. He couldn't speak.

The Stationmaster strode outside. He shut off the steam and surveyed his wrecked garden.

His wife picked up the plates. "You miserable engine," she scolded, "just look at our breakfast – covered in plaster. Now I shall have to cook some more." She banged the door behind her.

They finished their breakfast in the kitchen and left Thomas sulking on his own. More and more plaster fell. Thomas wanted to sneeze, but he didn't dare in case the house fell on top of him.

No one came near him for a very long time – everyone was much too busy. At last some workmen arrived to prop the house up with strong poles.

Next they brought a load of sleepers and made a road over the garden so that Donald and Douglas, puffing hard, could pull Thomas back to the rails again.

Thomas looked so comic that the twins laughed aloud. "Goodbye Thomas," they chuckled. "Don't forget your Driver next time!" His Driver and Fireman began to tidy him up. "You're a perfect disgrace," they told him. "We're ashamed of you."

"And so am I," said a voice behind them. "You're a very naughty engine," the Fat Controller continued. "Yes, Sir, I'm sorry, Sir," faltered Thomas.

"You must go to the Works to be mended, but they've no time for you now. Percy will take you to a siding where you can wait till they are ready."

Next day a diesel railcar came.
"That's Daisy," said the Fat Contoller. "She's come to do your
work. Diesels never run off to breakfast in Stationmasters' houses."
And he walked sternly away.

Thomas didn't enjoy his time at the Works. "It's nice to feel mended again," he said afterwards, "but they took so many of my old parts away and put new ones in, that I'm not sure whether I'm really me or another engine."

When Thomas came home, he soon made friends with Daisy. In fact, Thomas is glad to have her help with his passengers. He is now never so silly as to think he can manage without his Driver.